Under a Halloween Moon

Written and Illustrated by

Jennifer Cahill Tully

ISBN 978-0-9980531-0-3

First Printing, 2016

Jennifer Cahill Tully
Visit my website at www.halloweenmoon.co

Dedicated to all lovers of Halloween;
both young and old.

There is a *night*, of sheer *delight*

under a
Halloween
Moon

When indigo *skies* deceive your *eyes*,
the air will *glow* and soon you'll *know* you're

under a

Halloween Moon

With air so *crisp* and
breezes *brisk,*
the leaves will *crunch*
and children *bunch*

under a
Halloween Moon

Where tricks *abound*
and treats *astound*...

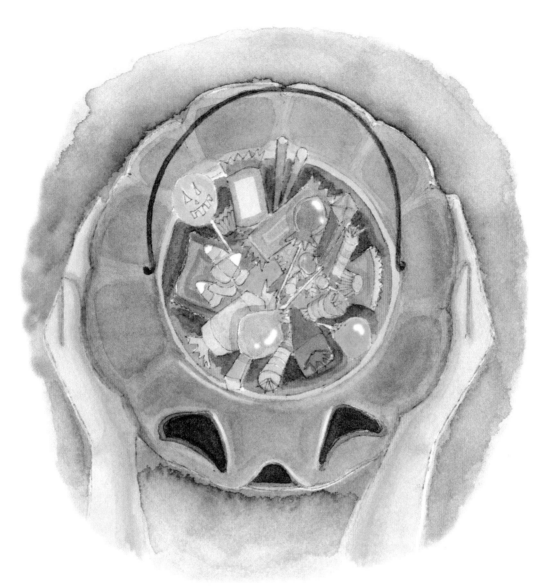

things might get *spooky*,
peculiar and *kooky*,

under a
Halloween Moon

Things might *confuse* you,
startle and *amuse* you . . .

shadows grow *longer*,
tensions grow *stronger*

under a
Halloween Moon

Wild creatures of *night*
will frolic in *flight,*

under a
Halloween Moon

Adventures are in *store*,
don't be afraid to *explore*

under a
Halloween Moon

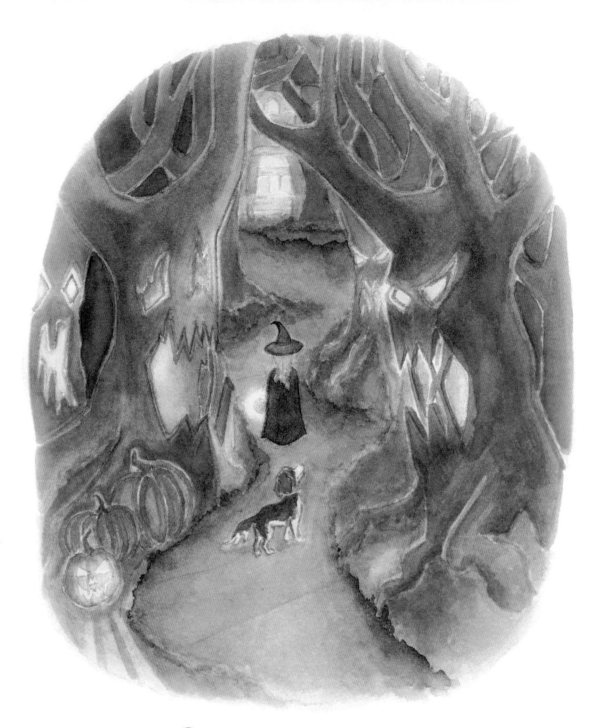

Odd things might *unravel*
on this night while you *travel*,

under a
$Halloween$ $Moon$

you might want to *retreat . . .*

from strange things that you *meet*,

under a
Halloween Moon

BOooo!

Potions will *bubble*, toil and *trouble*,
with visions so *eerie* one ought to be *leery*

under a
Halloween Moon

But don't let it *get you,*

trick and *upset you,*

just when it's most *hectic* and least *expected . . .*

That moon will *delight you,*
charm and *excite you*!

So get straight to the *fun,*
before the evening is *done*

For no night is as *thrilling*,
magic and *chilling* than...

under a
Halloween
Moon

Made in the USA
Lexington, KY
22 September 2016